HOUSTON
ROCKETS

by J Chris Roselius

Published by ABDO Publishing Company, 8000 West 78th Street, Edina, Minnesota 55439. Copyright © 2012 by Abdo Consulting Group, Inc. International copyrights reserved in all countries. No part of this book may be reproduced in any form without written permission from the publisher. SportsZone™ is a trademark and logo of ABDO Publishing Company.

Printed in the United States of America,
North Mankato, Minnesota
062011
092011

Editor: Dave McMahon
Copy Editor: Anna Comstock
Series design and cover production: Christa Schneider
Interior production: Carol Castro

Photo Credits: David J. Phillip/AP Images, cover, 1; Tim Johnson/AP Images, 4, 9, 26, 43 (top); Rick Bowmer/AP Images, 7, 30, 33; EFK/AP Images, 10, 42 (top); AP Images, 13, 14, 18, 20, 42 (middle); Martell/AP Images, 17; Lennox McLendon/AP Images, 23, 42 (bottom); Mike F. Kullen/AP Images, 25; Amy Sancetta/AP Images, 29; Rich Pedroncelli/AP Images, 34, 43 (middle); Gregory Smith/AP Images, 37; Eric Gay/AP Images, 38, 43 (bottom); Nam Y. Huh/AP Images, 41; John Raoux/AP Images, 44; Pat Sullivan/AP Images, 47

Library of Congress Cataloging-in-Publication Data
Roselius, J Chris.
  Houston Rockets / J Chris Roselius.
     p. cm. -- (Inside the NBA)
  Includes index.
  ISBN 978-1-61783-158-4
  1. Houston Rockets (Basketball team)--History--Juvenile literature. I. Title.
  GV885.52.H68R67 2012
  796.323'64097641411--dc23
                              2011021373

TABLE OF CONTENTS

CHAPTER 1

CLUTCH CITY

O nly weeks before the Houston Rockets began playing in the 1994 National Basketball Association (NBA) Finals, the Rockets were being looked down on by their own city.

The *Houston Chronicle* newspaper had the headline "Choke City" written at the top of the sports section earlier in the playoffs. Facing the Phoenix Suns in the Western Conference semifinals, Houston had blown an 18-point lead in Game 1. In Game 2, the Rockets led by 20 points in the fourth quarter, but Phoenix again came back. The Suns had escaped with a 124–117 win. That led to the "Choke City" headline in Houston.

Instead of being ahead two games to none in the series, the Rockets were down two games. And Games 3 and 4 were on the road in Phoenix.

"We traveled directly to Phoenix after [Game 2]," Rockets star center Hakeem Olajuwon said. "That was a

Rockets center Hakeem Olajuwon blocks the Phoenix Suns' A. C. Green's shot during the 1994 playoffs.

terrible flight. It was silent on the plane, as if somebody had died. Nobody was prepared for what had happened."

In Game 3, Vernon Maxwell scored 31 points in the second half to lead the Rockets to a 118–102 victory. Important points by teammates Mario Elie and rookie Sam Cassell allowed the Rockets to win both Games 3 and 4 to even the series.

Vernon Maxwell

Vernon Maxwell was a talented player for the Rockets. They got him in a trade with the San Antonio Spurs midway through the 1989–90 season. Maxwell became the starting shooting guard for the Rockets in his first full season with the team. He averaged at least 17 points per game during the next two seasons. On January 26, 1991, Maxwell scored 30 points in the fourth quarter against the Cleveland Cavaliers. He ended with 51 points that game. He also led the NBA in three-point field goals made in those two seasons. He made 172 three-pointers in 1990–91, and 162 in 1991–92.

Houston also won Game 5 109–86. But the Suns forced the series to go the distance with a 103–89 victory in Game 6 in Phoenix. The Rockets took advantage of the home crowd in Game 7 to win 104–94. They had advanced to the Western Conference finals for the first time since 1986.

There, the Utah Jazz was no match for Houston. The Rockets won the best-of-seven series in five games. They were off to play the New York Knicks in the Finals.

The Rockets had been to the Finals twice before, in 1981 and 1986. And both times, they had lost to the Boston Celtics in six games. The Knicks won Games 4 and 5 to take a 3–2 series lead. That caused fans to believe that Houston would once again fall short of a title.

But star center Hakeem Olajuwon had been named the

The Rockets' Hakeem Olajuwon posts up against New York Knicks center Patrick Ewing during Game 1 of the 1994 NBA Finals.

league's Most Valuable Player (MVP) for the 1993–94 season. And he made sure there would not be another failure. With the Rockets leading 84–82 in Game 6, Olajuwon stole a pass by Knicks guard John Starks. Knicks center Patrick Ewing then fouled him.

With the hometown Houston fans nervously watching, Olajuwon sank both free throws

Familiar Faces

When Houston faced New York in the 1994 NBA Finals, the series featured dominant centers Hakeem Olajuwon of Houston and Patrick Ewing of New York. The two players had also played against each other with a title on the line in the 1984 National Collegiate Athletic Association (NCAA) championship game. Ewing's Georgetown Hoyas defeated Olajuwon's Houston Cougars 84–75 in that game. But Olajuwon got even as the Rockets defeated the Knicks in seven games to win the NBA title.

SMILIN' SAM

During his rookie season with the Rockets, Sam Cassell became a key player, especially during the play-offs. The point guard from Florida State University played in 66 games and averaged 6.7 points and 2.9 assists during the 1993–94 regular season. He shot 42 percent from the field and 30 percent from behind the three-point line. But when the postseason started, Cassell stepped up his game. He averaged 9.4 points and 4.2 assists per game. He also made 38 percent of his three-point attempts and 87 percent of his free throws in the playoffs. While Cassell was busy making plays on the court, he usually did so with a smile. In fact, it was rare to not see a smile on his face. "He's Smilin' Sam," teammate Vernon Maxwell said. "He's the kind of guy who can miss eight shots in a row and still be just as confident that the ninth one is going in. You can't keep Sam Cassell down. He'll always come back to get you."

to give the Rockets an 86–82 lead. The Knicks scored to cut the lead to two. After the Rockets failed to score on their trip down the floor, the Knicks had a chance to win the game with their last shot. When play started after a break, Starks received a pass. He appeared to be open in the corner for a three-point shot that would win the game. But Olajuwon sprinted toward Starks. He blocked the shot to preserve the win and set up a Game 7.

"We are going to Game 7," Olajuwon said. "So close and so far. I'm going to take a little time tonight to digest this win. . . . But after all of the time, all of the games, all of the years, this is the one game I've wanted to play."

With Olajuwon leading the way in Game 7, the Rockets earned a 90–84 victory and their first NBA

Just weeks after being labeled "Choke City," Houston was "Clutch City," home to the 1994 NBA champion Rockets.

championship. As Houston celebrated its first major sports title, Olajuwon was mobbed by his teammates. Ten years after being drafted by the Rockets, the veteran center scored 25 points in Game 7. He averaged 26.9 points, 9.9 rebounds, 3.9 blocks, and 2.9 assists per game against the Knicks and was named the NBA Finals MVP.

"The team has worked hard all year for the honor of being champions and the team as a whole, as a unit, deserved the title," Olajuwon said.

Now, the Rockets were calling Houston "Clutch City."

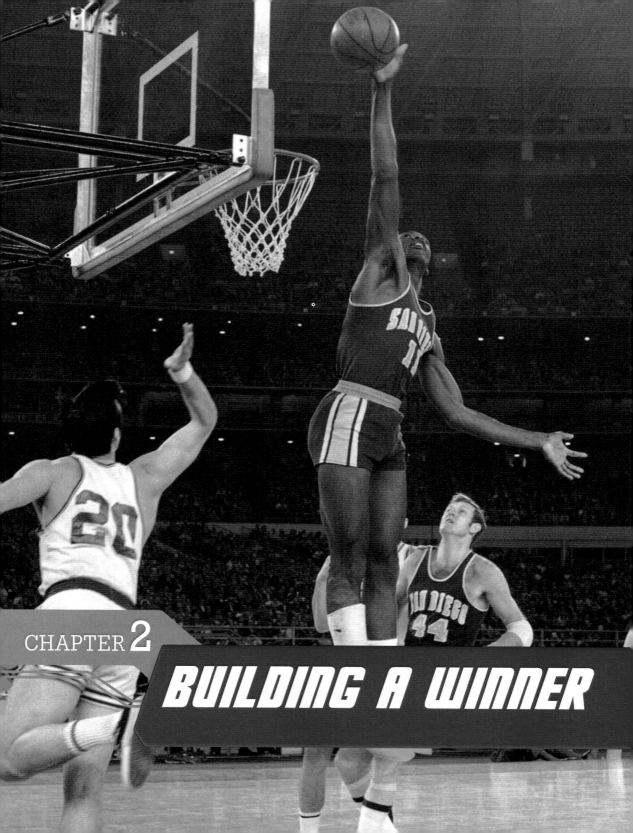

CHAPTER 2

BUILDING A WINNER

The Houston Rockets have made four trips to the NBA Finals through 2010–11, and they have won the championship twice. But the Rockets wish they could forget about the 1967–68 season. That was their first season in the league.

Playing as an expansion team in San Diego, California, the club won just 15 games and lost 67. That was a league record for losses at the time. The Rockets suffered through a 17-game losing streak that season. The streak ended when they defeated the Philadelphia 76ers 111–106 on February 16, 1968. San Diego then finished the season with a 15-game losing streak. From January 18 through the end of the season, the Rockets won only one of their final 33 games.

The Rockets and the Baltimore Bullets were the two worst teams in the league that season. The Rockets won a coin

The San Diego Rockets' Elvin Hayes leaps to block a shot from the Boston Celtics' Larry Siegfried during a 1969 game.

Calvin Murphy

Calvin Murphy was only 5 feet 8 inches tall and weighed just 165 pounds. Even so, Murphy showed everyone he belonged in the NBA in 1993 as he was inducted into the Basketball Hall of Fame. His 17,949 career points ranked second in Rockets history through 2010–11, behind only Hakeem Olajuwon. Murphy is one of only five Rocket players to have his number (No. 23) retired.

flip with Baltimore to pick first in the NBA Draft. The Rockets selected Elvin Hayes from the University of Houston with their first pick.

Hayes was outstanding for the Rockets during his rookie season. He led the team in both scoring and rebounding with an average of 28.4 points and 17.1 rebounds per game. Don Kojis and John Block joined Hayes to help San Diego improve by 22 games that season. The Rockets finished 37–45 and made

the playoffs. They lost to the Atlanta Hawks in the Western Division semifinals.

With Hayes at center, the Rockets added two more stand-outs in the 1970 draft, selecting forward Rudy Tomjanovich and guard Calvin Murphy.

But the young Rockets still struggled to win. After the 1970–71 season, Houston businessmen Wayne Duddleston and Billy Goldberg bought the franchise and moved it to Houston.

The Rockets were only 34–48 in 1971–72 during their first year in Houston. After the season, Hayes was traded to the Baltimore Bullets because he and coach Tex Winter had disagreements. Houston suffered through two more losing seasons before going 41–41 in 1974–75 to finally make the playoffs. It was the first time the Rockets had not had a

Rockets guard Calvin Murphy tries to keep the ball away from
Philadelphia 76ers defender Hal Greer during a 1971 game.

losing season in team history. It was also the first time they had earned a spot in the postseason.

Murphy and Tomjanovich led the team to the Eastern Conference semifinals. Murphy was an outstanding scorer from outside. "Rudy T.," as Tomjanovich was nicknamed, was a top scorer and rebounder. Mike Newlin also played a key role for Houston. He averaged more than 14 points per game.

Houston slipped to 40–42 in 1975–76. That season also was the first in The Summit, their new arena. The Rockets missed the playoffs that season. But it was obvious that with Murphy, Tomjanovich, and Newlin, the team had talent. And during the offseason, the Rockets made a trade that would change the future.

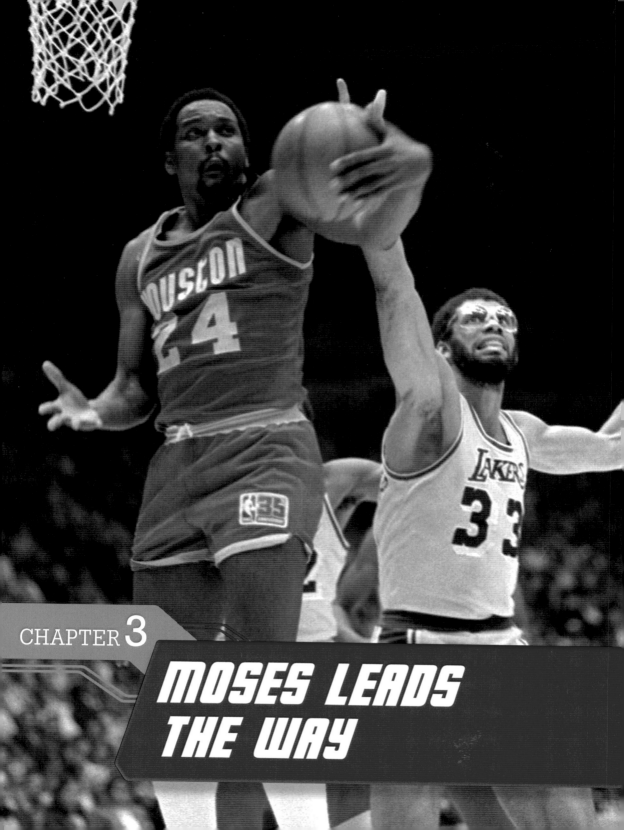

CHAPTER 3

MOSES LEADS
THE WAY

In 1974, Moses Malone made history by skipping college and signing with the Utah Stars of the American Basketball Association (ABA). At just 19 years old, he averaged 18.8 points and 14.6 rebounds per game for the Stars.

When the ABA closed after the 1975–76 season, Malone ended up with the NBA's Portland Trail Blazers. Portland then traded him to the Buffalo Braves.

But the Rockets badly wanted Malone. Team officials believed he would fit in perfectly with Calvin Murphy, Rudy Tomjanovich, and Mike Newlin. So Houston traded two first-round draft choices to Buffalo for Malone.

Malone averaged 13.5 points and 13.1 rebounds per game during the 1976–77 season with the Rockets. Tomjanovich had averages of 21.6 points and 8.4 rebounds per game. Murphy averaged 17.9 points per game and Newlin

The Rockets' Moses Malone grabs the ball from Los Angeles Lakers star Kareem Abdul-Jabbar during a 1981 game.

averaged 12.7 points per game. Rookie guard John Lucas also contributed. Lucas averaged 11.1 points and 5.6 assists per game.

The Rockets won 49 games that season to set a team record for wins. They also won the Central Division title. That meant they did not have to play in the first round of the playoffs. In the second round, the Rockets took on Elvin Hayes and the Washington Bullets. Malone proved he could handle Hayes, and the Rockets eliminated the Bullets in six games. But in the Eastern Conference finals, Houston lost to the Philadelphia 76ers in six games.

Many believed the Rockets would be better during the 1977–78 season. But on December 9, 1977, their campaign took a turn for the worse. Kevin Kunnert, the Rockets' 7-foot center, got into a

Rudy T.

Rudy Tomjanovich played 11 seasons for the Rockets, averaging 17.4 points and 8.1 rebounds per game for his career. Rudy T., as he was nicknamed, was an All-Star five times before he retired in 1981. He was hired as the Rockets' coach midway through the 1991–92 season.

fight with Kermit Washington of the Los Angeles Lakers. Tomjanovich was not part of the fight. But as he rushed up the court, Washington turned and punched him.

In an instant, Tomjanovich was on the floor. Blood spilled from his head. Tomjanovich suffered massive injuries—the punch had shattered bones in his face. Amazingly, Tomjanovich did not realize how injured he was until doctors later explained the injuries to him.

Tomjanovich missed the rest of the season. Malone also missed 23 games due to

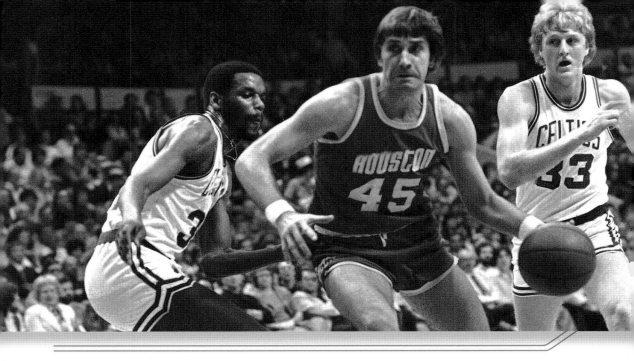

Rockets forward Rudy Tomjanovich drives through Boston Celtics defenders during a 1980 playoff game.

an injury. The Rockets were unable to overcome the loss of both players and finished the season just 28–54.

Tomjanovich returned to action in 1978–79. He averaged 19 points and 7.7 rebounds per game. Murphy scored an average of 20.2 points per game that season. And a healthy Malone dominated the league. He was named the league's MVP after he averaged 24.8 points and a

league-leading 17.6 rebounds per game. The Rockets finished the season 47–35, but their playoff run ended quickly. The Atlanta Hawks knocked them out in the first round.

Del Harris replaced coach Tom Nissalke after the season. He guided the Rockets to a 41–41 record in 1979–80. Houston defeated the San Antonio Spurs in the first round of the postseason, but then fell to the

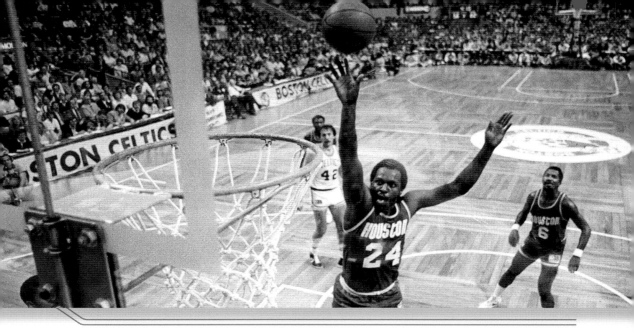

Rockets center/forward Moses Malone releases the ball for two of his 31 points during a 1981 game against the Boston Celtics.

Boston Celtics in the Eastern Conference semifinals.

The new Dallas Mavericks team joined the NBA for the 1980–81 season. That sent the Rockets to the Midwest Division of the Western Conference. Houston struggled to be consistent and finished 40–42. But they would go on a winning streak in the postseason to earn their first trip to the Finals.

The Rockets faced the defending champion Los Angeles Lakers in the opening round of the playoffs. The Rockets shocked the Lakers by winning Game 1 in Los Angeles. The Lakers won Game 2 in Houston, but the Rockets took Game 3 89–86. That victory allowed them to advance to the conference semifinals against San Antonio and Spurs star player George Gervin.

The series was decided in Game 7. The Rockets pulled off their second straight playoff

Moses Malone

Moses Malone was a 12-time All-Star and a three-time MVP. In addition, he was named one of the 50 Greatest Players in NBA history in 1996. But what Malone might be best known for was his fierce rebounding ability, especially on the offensive end of the court. In 1976–77, his first season with the Rockets, he grabbed 437 offensive rebounds. Those are rebounds he secured after one of his teammates missed a shot. That set an NBA record and broke the previous mark of 365 offensive rebounds in a single season. During the 1978–79 season, Malone grabbed 587 offensive rebounds (7.2 per game) to shatter his own record.

upset with a 105–100 win in San Antonio.

Up next were the Western Conference finals, with the Rockets facing the equally surprising Kansas City Kings. The Kings had also finished the regular season 40–42. But Malone and the Rockets easily handled the Kings in five games. Houston's magical run ended in the NBA Finals against Boston. The series was tied at two games apiece. But Larry Bird, Robert Parish, and Cedric Maxwell guided the Celtics to victories in Games 5 and 6 to prevent the Rockets from winning their first title.

Elvin Hayes rejoined the Rockets in 1981–82. He teamed with Malone to lead Houston to 46 wins. However, they were knocked out of the playoffs in the first round. Malone was again named the league's MVP. He averaged 31.1 points per game and 14.7 rebounds per game to lead the league in rebounding for the second straight season. After the season, however, Malone became a free agent. Unable to match his contract demands, the Rockets traded Malone to the Philadelphia 76ers. And just like that, the Moses Malone era came to a sudden close.

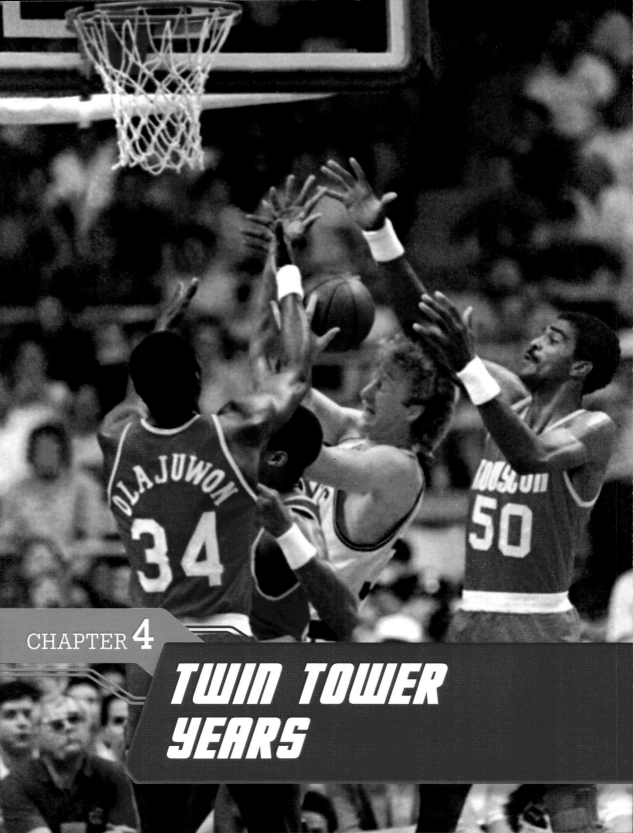

CHAPTER **4**

TWIN TOWER YEARS

Rudy Tomjanovich had retired and Calvin Murphy was no longer the scorer he once was. But the loss of Moses Malone devastated the Rockets. Houston dropped in the standings and finished the 1982–83 season with a 14–68 record—the worst in the league.

Bill Fitch replaced Harris as coach after the season. Fitch had guided the Boston Celtics to a league title in 1981 by defeating the Rockets in the Finals. With the first pick in the 1983 NBA Draft, the Rockets selected 7-foot-4 center Ralph Sampson from Virginia. Sampson had a fantastic rookie season. He averaged 21 points, 11.1 rebounds, and 2.4 blocks per game to be named NBA Rookie of the Year. Fellow

Rockets teammates Hakeem Olajuwon, *left*, and Ralph Sampson, *right*, were known as the Twin Towers during their time together from 1984–85 through 1987–88.

rookie Rodney McCray averaged 10.8 points per game for the Rockets and young forward Lewis Lloyd scored 17.8 points per game. Guard Robert Reid was in the midst of his standout 10-year career with Houston, as well.

While the young Rockets improved, they still went only 29–53. That was the worst record in the Western Conference. For the second straight season, they flipped a coin for the top pick in the draft. The

Robert Reid

Robert Reid's specialty on the court was his ability to play defense. During the Rockets' 1981 playoff run, he averaged more than one block and two steals per game. He was also assigned to defend the opponent's best player, such as Magic Johnson of the Los Angeles Lakers and Larry Bird of the Boston Celtics. Reid was also versatile. Because of injuries, he switched to point guard during the 1986 playoffs, but still helped the Rockets reach the NBA Finals.

Rockets won the coin flip and selected Hakeem Olajuwon out of the University of Houston.

With Sampson and Olajuwon, the Rockets were set to start two 7-foot players at the same time. Thus came the beginning of the "Twin Towers." Olajuwon played center for Houston because he could better handle the demands of playing close to the basket. Sampson, despite his height, could handle the ball and had a solid jump shot. That allowed him to play outside and face the basket. For opposing teams, it was a matchup that was tough to defend.

"I think that they're a new phenomenon," said Rockets general manager Ray Patterson.

With the Twin Towers, the Rockets improved by 19 games in the 1984–85 season. Sampson proved his Rookie of the Year season was no fluke.

Rockets teammates surround Ralph Sampson after he scored the winning basket to send the team to the 1986 NBA Finals

He averaged 22.1 points, 10.4 rebounds, and two blocked shots per game that season. And Olajuwon immediately showed he could exist with Sampson. Olajuwon, nicknamed "The Dream," averaged 20.6 points, 11.9 rebounds, and 2.7 blocked shots per game. The Rockets returned to the playoffs that season after a two-year absence, but lost in the first round.

In the 1985–86 season, Sampson and Olajuwon guided Houston to a 51–31 record and a trip to the postseason.

Olajuwon averaged 23.5 points, 11.5 rebounds, 3.4 blocks, and two steals per game. Sampson scored 18.9 points and grabbed 11.1 rebounds per game on average. Teammates Lloyd, John Lucas, Robert Reid, and McCray all averaged more than 10 points per game, as well.

Houston swept the Sacramento Kings in the first round of the playoffs. Then, the Rockets won the Western Conference semifinals against the Denver Nuggets in six games. And in the Western Conference finals, Houston was too fast and too athletic for the Los Angeles Lakers. The Rockets won the series in five games to advance to the NBA Finals to face the Celtics.

"We're going to Boston with confidence," Sampson said. "We are not just happy to be going there. We're going there intent on winning the series."

The Rockets were picked by many to win the title. But the veteran Celtics proved that age has its advantages. The Celtics slowed Sampson and Olajuwon thanks to the defense of Robert Parish and Kevin McHale. And the Rockets had no answer for Boston's Larry Bird, who helped the Celtics win the series in six games.

With Sampson and Olajuwon in the prime of their careers, the Rockets still figured to become one of the dominant teams in the NBA. But that was assuming both players remained healthy.

Sampson played in only 43 games in 1986–87, slowed

Rockets players, *from left*, Hakeem Olajuwon, Robert Reid, Ralph Sampson, and Mitchell Wiggins react during Houston's Game 1 loss in the 1986 NBA Finals.

by injuries to his knees and ankles. His averages dropped to 15.6 points and 8.7 rebounds per game. The Rockets fell to 42–40 and lost in the conference semifinals. Sampson, who was rumored to have been clashing with Fitch, was traded to the Golden State Warriors during the 1987–88 season. The Rockets received Joe Barry Carroll and Sleepy Floyd in return.

The Twin Towers, expected to help the Rockets dominate the league, lasted less than four years. And the title Houston fans had hoped for would have to wait a few more years.

CHAPTER 5

THE HEART OF A CHAMPION

Ralph Sampson might have been gone, but the Rockets still had Hakeem Olajuwon. And with him, they won 46 games during the 1987–88 season. But after the club was ousted in the first round of the playoffs, Don Chaney replaced Bill Fitch as coach.

Under Chaney's guidance, the Rockets continued to win. They made the playoffs in each of his first three seasons. But Houston was unable to advance past the first round in any of those seasons. They missed the postseason completely in 1992. Former Rocket Rudy Tomjanovich replaced Chaney after 52 games in the 1991–92 season. The new coach went 16–14 to end the campaign.

The Rockets kept Tomjanovich as their coach after the season. They were entering the best stretch of play in team history, beginning with

The Rockets' Hakeem Olajuwon rises above Dallas Mavericks defenders for a basket during the 1988 playoffs.

the 1992–93 season. Tomjanovich had a great relationship with Olajuwon and made sure to surround him with the right players. In his first full season as coach, Tomjanovich led the Rockets to 55 wins and an appearance in the conference semifinals.

Olajuwon averaged 26.1 points, 13 rebounds, and 4.2 blocks per game. Forward Otis Thorpe also was reliable. He averaged 12.8 points and 8.2 rebounds per game. In addition, Robert Horry, Kenny Smith, and Vernon Maxwell played well. The Rockets then broke

through during the 1993–94 season and won their first NBA title. Olajuwon won the league's MVP Award.

During the 1994–95 season, team officials believed the Rockets needed to make player changes if the team was going to repeat as champion. On February 14, 1995, the Rockets traded Thorpe to the Portland Trail Blazers for Clyde Drexler. The Rockets also gave up other players and draft picks.

Drexler had been a star with Olajuwon when they were teammates at the University of Houston. The Rockets wanted Drexler to provide an extra push for the playoffs. With Drexler's ability to shoot from the outside and drive to the basket, opposing teams could not simply focus on guarding Olajuwon.

Houston was the sixth seed entering the 1995 postseason. Facing the Utah Jazz in the first

Rockets coach Rudy Tomjanovich talks with point guard Sam Cassell during the 1994 NBA Finals.

round, the Rockets fell behind two games to one in the series. They won 123–106 in Game 4, as Drexler scored 41 points and Olajuwon 40. Houston then defeated the Jazz 95–91 on the road in Game 5, winning the series. The Olajuwon-Drexler duo had come through again. Olajuwon had 33 points and 10 rebounds. Drexler added 31 points and 10 rebounds.

In a rematch of the 1994 Western Conference semifinals,

Help Coming

"What more could he ask for? He wasn't happy with what was going on here and he's going back home. He gives them somebody who's one of the top go-to players in the league. He's a clutch player who's really going to help Houston."
—Portland guard Rod Strickland commenting on the trade that sent Clyde Drexler to the Houston Rockets

The Rockets' Hakeem Olajuwon, *left*, and Clyde Drexler, *right*, celebrate a Houston victory over the Phoenix Suns during the 1995 playoffs.

the Rockets took on the Phoenix Suns. The Suns dominated the first two games, which they won by 22 and 24 points respectively. Houston then won Game 3 but lost Game 4. The Suns led three games to one and were just one victory away from advancing to the conference finals. Only four teams had ever been able to overcome a deficit that large. Boston had last done it in 1981.

"It won't happen," Phoenix forward A. C. Green said after being asked if the Suns could blow a three-games-to-one lead. "That's the way I look at it. I'm sure there are people who will come up with some kind of scenario where it could happen. But it's not going to happen."

But Suns guard Kevin Johnson was not ready to look ahead to the conference finals.

"The Rockets have the heart of a champion," he said.

Houston was not at full strength for Game 5, with Drexler battling the flu. But Olajuwon sent the game into overtime when he drained a jump hook shot with eight seconds remaining. Houston took the momentum and pulled away for a 103–97 victory to stay alive in the series.

The Rockets then won Game 6 in Houston to force a Game 7 in Phoenix. Houston fell behind by 10 points in the first half but rallied in the second half. With the score tied 110–110, Mario Elie took a pass from Robert Horry in the corner and sank a three-pointer with 7.1 seconds left to give the Rockets a 113–110 lead. As Phoenix called timeout, Elie turned and blew a goodbye kiss to the crowd. The shot propelled the Rockets to a

ROBERT HORRY

Robert Horry played the first four of his 16 seasons with the Rockets. He won seven NBA titles during his career—two with Houston, three with the Los Angeles Lakers, and two with the San Antonio Spurs.

A solid defender and good outside shooter, Horry earned the nickname "Big Shot Bob" for his ability to hit the big shot when needed most. One of those came in Game 3 of the 1995 NBA Finals against the Orlando Magic. With the clock winding down and the score tied 103–103, Hakeem Olajuwon passed to Horry. He fired a three-pointer over the outstretched hands of Horace Grant. It went in, giving Houston a 106–103 win and a 3–0 series lead.

Horry was consistent throughout the Finals, averaging 17.8 points, 10 rebounds, and 3.8 assists per game. In Game 2, he set an NBA Finals record with seven steals as the Rockets won 117–106.

115–114 win and a surprising berth in the conference finals.

"Dream was wide open, but I had my feet set. I let it go and it felt good," Elie said.

The Rockets had one more hurdle to overcome if they wanted to play for their second straight title. The San Antonio Spurs featured league MVP David Robinson, and the Spurs had finished the regular season with 62 wins to lead the league. The Rockets won the first two games of the series in San Antonio, but the Spurs won the next two games in Houston.

Before the start of Game 5, Robinson was honored during a pregame MVP award ceremony. That must have inspired Olajuwon. Many felt Olajuwon could have won the award himself for a second straight season. Showing Robinson every move he had, Olajuwon scored 42 points to lead the Rockets to a 111–90

win. Robinson scored just 22 points. The Rockets then won Game 6 100–95 in Houston to earn a repeat trip to the Finals, where they would face the Orlando Magic.

Orlando had won 57 games during the regular season behind the inside play of Shaquille O'Neal and outside shooting of Penny Hardaway. But the young Magic was no match for Houston as the Rockets swept Orlando in four games to claim their second straight title. Olajuwon was

Rockets forward Robert Horry celebrates with the 1995 NBA championship trophy after his team defeated the Orlando Magic.

named the Finals MVP, and the Rockets made history by being the first team to win four play-off series against teams with 50 or more wins.

"Nobody has ever done what this team has done . . . come from the sixth seed . . . down in the series," Tomjano-vich said as the Rockets were presented with their second straight Larry O'Brien Trophy as league champions. "We had nonbelievers all along the way. I have one thing to say to those nonbelievers: Don't ever underestimate the heart of a champion."

CHAPTER 6

IN SEARCH OF ANOTHER TITLE

With the careers of both Hakeem Olajuwon and Clyde Drexler coming to an end, the Rockets did everything they could to win another title. After the Seattle SuperSonics knocked them out of the playoffs in 1996, the Rockets traded four players to the Phoenix Suns for forward Charles Barkley.

Included in those four were Sam Cassell and Robert Horry. They both had played important roles on the Rockets' championship teams. The Rockets were hoping that Olajuwon, Drexler, and Barkley would lead the team to another championship.

The Rockets won 57 games during the 1996–97 regular season. They swept the Minnesota Timberwolves in the first round of the playoffs. They then defeated Seattle in seven games to advance to the conference finals against the Utah

Rockets forward Charles Barkley goes up for a shot against the Sacramento Kings during a 1996 game.

STEVE FRANCIS

The Rockets expected Steve Francis to become the team's next star and lead Houston to several NBA titles. Despite being an outstanding player, he was never quite able to live up to those expectations.

Francis was named the NBA's Co-Rookie of the Year in 2000 and was an All-Star from 2002 to 2004. During the 2003–04 season, Francis averaged 16.6 points, 5.5 rebounds, and 6.2 assists per game. He became only the fourth player in NBA history to average at least 15 points, five rebounds, and five assists in each of his first five seasons in the league.

During his tenure with the Rockets, Francis's only playoff appearance came in 2004 when the Los Angeles Lakers eliminated Houston in the first round. After the season, the Rockets traded Francis and two other players to the Orlando Magic for Tracy McGrady and three other players.

Jazz. The Jazz had finished the season with 64 wins.

Utah won the first two games of the series at home before the Rockets won Games 3 and 4 in Houston. But Utah then won Games 5 and 6 in Houston to end the Rockets' season.

Injuries ruined the 1997–98 season for the Rockets. Olajuwon was limited to 47 games and Barkley played in only 68. Drexler also missed 12 games. Houston still managed to make the playoffs with a 41–41 record, but lost to Utah in the first round in five games.

When Drexler retired after the season, the Rockets got Scottie Pippen from the Chicago Bulls in a trade. But the trade did not lead to a title as the Los Angeles Lakers eliminated the Rockets in the first round of the playoffs.

Rockets point guard Steve Francis drives past Atlanta Hawks defender Mark Strickland during a 2002 game.

Pippen and Barkley did not always get along, either, and Pippen was traded to the Portland Trail Blazers during the offseason.

Houston then brought in rookie point guard Steve Francis. He came from the Vancouver Grizzlies after the draft to run the offense and pass the ball to Olajuwon and Barkley.

But Barkley injured his left knee early in the season and played in only 20 games. The Rockets finished the season 34–48. That was their worst record since the 1983–84.

Barkley retired at the end of the season and Olajuwon played just one more season for Houston. He was traded to the Toronto Raptors in August

Rockets center Yao Ming guards San Antonio Spurs center David Robinson during Yao's NBA debut in October 2002.

2001. Olajuwon played one season for the Raptors before he retired. With Francis injured for part of the 2001–02 season, Houston finished only 28–54.

The Rockets won the draft lottery and received the first pick in the 2002 NBA Draft. With it, the Rockets selected 7-foot-6 center Yao Ming of China. The selection made Yao the first foreign player to be picked first overall.

Francis and an inexperienced Yao were unable to bring the Rockets back to the playoffs from 2001 to 2003. They did have a winning record in two of those three seasons, though.

After the 2002–03 season, Tomjanovich stepped down as coach. He was replaced by Jeff

Van Gundy. The club returned to the playoffs, but was eliminated in the first round. That offseason, the Rockets traded Francis to the Orlando Magic for Tracy McGrady in a deal that included multiple players. McGrady, a 6-foot-8 forward, was one of the top scorers in the league.

The Rockets finished 51–31 in McGrady's first season in Houston. But once again the team was knocked out in the first round of the playoffs. In 2005–06, McGrady played in only 47 games and Yao played in only 57 as the Rockets finished 34–48. Yao was again injured the following season, but a healthy McGrady led the Rockets to a 52–30 record. However, Houston once again failed to get past the first round of the playoffs.

The Rockets hired Rick Adelman as head coach for the 2007–08 season, and they started strong. They won 12 games in a row and had a 36–20 record. But on February 24, 2008, Yao suffered another injury. That made it the third consecutive year that his season had ended early because of an injury. Yao had averaged 22 points and 11 rebounds per game that season.

Despite the loss of Yao, the Rockets won another 10 consecutive games. That gave them a 22-game winning streak, which was the second-longest in NBA history. The streak finally came to an end when Boston defeated the Rockets on March 18, 2008.

Houston Rockets center/forward Chuck Hayes, known as a strong rebounder and defensive player, and 41-year-old veteran center Dikembe Mutombo had filled in for Yao. Houston ended the season with 55 wins, but the Rockets again failed to advance past the first round of the playoffs. It was the sixth straight time Houston was eliminated in the first round. Yao returned for the 2008–09 season, and for the first time in four years he played the entire season. Houston won 53 games and finally got past the first round of the playoffs by beating Portland.

Next, the Rockets faced the Lakers. They split the first four games of the series. However, bad luck struck once again as Yao suffered yet another foot injury near the end of Game 3. With their big center out of action, the Rockets lost Game 5 118–78. Houston pulled out a victory in Game 6, but in Game 7 in Los Angeles, the Lakers defeated the Rockets 89–70 to take the series.

Yao's foot injury eventually required surgery. He had to miss the entire 2009–10 season. And McGrady was limited to six games that season due to a knee injury. He was traded to the New York Knicks in February 2010 and played

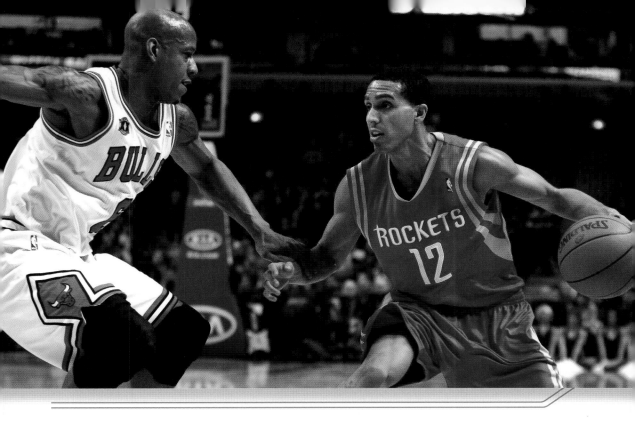

Rockets guard Kevin Martin looks to make a play against the Chicago Bulls in 2010. He led the Rockets with 23.5 points per game in 2010–11.

in 24 games for them. Without Yao and McGrady, guard Aaron Brooks and forward Luis Scola, each in his third season, led the Rockets to a 42–40 record.

The Rockets improved in 2010–11. However, that improvement was small. They won one more game than the previous year to finish 43–39, and missed the playoffs for the second straight year. Suffering through injuries, Yao played in only five games. Hoping for improvement behind guard Kevin Martin, who led the team with 23.5 points per game in 2010–11, the Rockets fired Adelman after the season. Fans hope a new coach can lead them back to the playoffs and, eventually, to another NBA title.

TIMELINE

1968	The San Diego Rockets draft Elvin Hayes of the University of Houston with the first pick of the NBA Draft on June 4.
1972	The Rockets relocate to Houston after four seasons in San Diego.
1976	Houston selects University of Maryland guard John Lucas with the first pick of the NBA Draft on June 8. Houston acquires center Moses Malone from the Buffalo Braves on October 24.
1979	Malone is named the NBA's MVP. During the season, he averaged 24.8 points and a league-leading 17.6 rebounds per game.
1981	The Rockets advance to the NBA Finals for the first time, but lose to the Boston Celtics in six games.
1982	Malone earns his second MVP award after averaging 31.1 points and a league-leading 14.7 rebounds per game.
1983	Houston selects Ralph Sampson of Virginia with the first overall pick of the NBA Draft on June 28.
1984	Sampson is named the Rookie of Year after averaging 21 points and 11.1 rebounds per game. The Rockets take Hakeem Olajuwon of the University of Houston with the first pick of the NBA Draft on June 19.
1986	Houston advances to the NBA Finals, but once again falls short of the title, losing to Boston in six games.

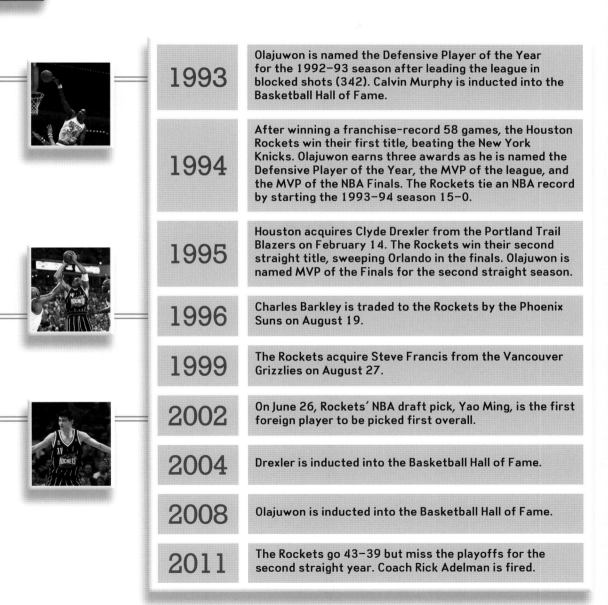

1993	Olajuwon is named the Defensive Player of the Year for the 1992–93 season after leading the league in blocked shots (342). Calvin Murphy is inducted into the Basketball Hall of Fame.
1994	After winning a franchise-record 58 games, the Houston Rockets win their first title, beating the New York Knicks. Olajuwon earns three awards as he is named the Defensive Player of the Year, the MVP of the league, and the MVP of the NBA Finals. The Rockets tie an NBA record by starting the 1993–94 season 15–0.
1995	Houston acquires Clyde Drexler from the Portland Trail Blazers on February 14. The Rockets win their second straight title, sweeping Orlando in the finals. Olajuwon is named MVP of the Finals for the second straight season.
1996	Charles Barkley is traded to the Rockets by the Phoenix Suns on August 19.
1999	The Rockets acquire Steve Francis from the Vancouver Grizzlies on August 27.
2002	On June 26, Rockets' NBA draft pick, Yao Ming, is the first foreign player to be picked first overall.
2004	Drexler is inducted into the Basketball Hall of Fame.
2008	Olajuwon is inducted into the Basketball Hall of Fame.
2011	The Rockets go 43–39 but miss the playoffs for the second straight year. Coach Rick Adelman is fired.

QUICK STATS

FRANCHISE HISTORY

San Diego Rockets (1967–71)
Houston Rockets (1971–)

NBA FINALS
(wins in bold)

1981, 1986, **1994**, **1995**

CONFERENCE FINALS

1977, 1981, 1986, 1994, 1995, 1997

KEY PLAYERS
(position[s]; years with team)

Charles Barkley (F; 1996–2000)
Aaron Brooks (G; 2007–11)
Clyde Drexler (F/G; 1995–98)
Steve Francis (G; 1999–2004, 2007)
Elvin Hayes (C; 1968–72, 1981–84)
Robert Horry (F; 1992–96)

John Lucas (G; 1976–78, 1984–86,
    1989–90)
Moses Malone (C; 1976–82)
Tracy McGrady (G/F; 2004–10)
Calvin Murphy (G; 1970–83)
Mike Newlin (F/G; 1971–79)
Hakeem Olajuwon (F/C; 1984–01)
Robert Reid (F/G; 1977–88)
Ralph Sampson (C; 1984–87)
Kenny Smith (G; 1990–96)
Rudy Tomjanovich (F; 1970–81)
Yao Ming (C; 2002–09, 2010–)

KEY COACHES

Rick Adelman (2007–11):
    193–135; 9–10 (postseason)
Bill Fitch (1983–88):
    216–194; 21–18 (postseason)
Rudy Tomjanovich (1992–03):
    503–397; 51–39 (postseason)
Jeff Van Gundy (2003–07):
    182–146; 7–12 (postseason)

HOME ARENAS

San Diego Sports Arena (1967–71)
Hofheinz Pavilion (1971–75)
HemisFair Arena (1972–73, 12
    games)
The Summit (1975–03)
—Known as Compaq Center
    (1997–03)
Toyota Center (2003–)

* All statistics through 2010–11 season

QUOTES AND ANECDOTES

"My passion for fashion has been there from the beginning. I've designed so many cool, nice clothes for myself that you want to take that public." —Hakeem Olajuwon on the clothing line he started after his playing career ended

The NBA instituted the NBA Draft Lottery system after the Rockets won back-to-back coin flips. The Rockets drafted Ralph Sampson and Hakeem Olajuwon first in 1983 and 1984.

Rick Barry joined the Rockets in 1978. He had always worn No. 24, but Moses Malone had already taken that number. So Barry came up with a unique solution. He got permission from the league to wear No. 2 at home and No. 4 on the road.

"He's like a baseball pitcher who's trying to throw seven or eight different pitches. Right now he just has to concentrate and master three or four things instead of doing everything. It'll take a little time." —Pete Newell, then with the Golden State Warriors, talking about center Ralph Sampson and his need to focus on only a few of this talents

"Look at this team. Kenny's [guard Kenny Smith] been traded a couple of times, OT [forward Otis Thorpe] has been traded, San Antonio just about gave me away, and that's three of our starters. There are probably people around the league who are wondering how we ever turned into a championship team. Well, Rudy T. is a big part of the answer." —Rockets guard Vernon Maxwell praising head coach Rudy Tomjanovich after the Rockets won their first title in 1994

GLOSSARY

assist

A pass that leads directly to a made basket.

berth

A place, spot, or position, such as in the NBA playoffs.

contender

A team that is in the race for a championship or playoff berth.

contract

A binding agreement about, for example, years of commitment by a basketball player in exchange for a given salary.

draft

A system used by professional sports leagues to select new players in order to spread incoming talent among all teams. The NBA Draft is held each June.

expansion

In sports, the addition of a franchise or franchises to a league.

franchise

An entire sports organization, including the players, coaches, and staff.

free agent

A player whose contract has expired and who is able to sign with a team of his choice.

general manager

The executive who is in charge of the team's overall operation. He or she hires and fires coaches, drafts players, and signs free agents.

overtime

A period in a basketball game that is played to determine a winner when the four quarters end in a tie.

postseason

The games in which the best teams play after the regular-season schedule has been completed.

rebound

To secure the basketball after a missed shot.

FOR MORE INFORMATION

Further Reading

Ballard, Chris. *The Art of a Beautiful Game: The Thinking Fan's Tour of the NBA*. New York: Simon & Schuster, 2009.

Feinstein, Jon. *The Punch: One Night, Two Lives, and the Fight That Changed Basketball Forever*. Boston: Little, Brown & Co., 2002.

Tomjanovich, Rudy, with Robert Falkoff. *A Rocket at Heart: My Life and My Team*. New York: Simon & Schuster, 1997.

Web Links

To learn more about the Houston Rockets, visit ABDO Publishing Company online at **www.abdopublishing.com**. Web sites about the Rockets are featured on our Book Links page. These links are routinely monitored and updated to provide the most current information available.

Places to Visit

Hofheinz Pavilion
University of Houston
4800 Calhoun Road
Houston, TX 77004
713-743-2255
www.uhcougars.com/facilities/hou-hofheinz.html
This was the home of the Rockets from 1971 to 1975 after they relocated from San Diego.

Naismith Memorial Basketball Hall of Fame
1000 West Columbus Avenue
Springfield, MA 01105
413-781-6500
www.hoophall.com
This hall of fame and museum highlights the greatest players and moments in the history of basketball. Moses Malone and Hakeem Olajuwon are among the former Rockets players enshrined here.

Toyota Center
1510 Polk Street
Houston, TX 77002
713-758-7200
www.houstontoyotacenter.com
This has been home to the Rockets since 2003. The team plays 41 regular-season games here each year. Tours are available when the Rockets are not playing.

INDEX

About the Author

J Chris Roselius is an award-winning journalist and writer. A graduate of the University of Texas, he has written numerous books. Currently residing in Houston, Texas, he enjoys spending time with his wife and two children. When not attending baseball games with them, he also likes to watch a variety of sports, on either the professional or collegiate level.